Crayola Kids Adventures
the Trojan Horse

BASED ON THE CRAYOLA® KIDS ADVENTURES™ VIDEO
ADAPTED BY JUSTINE KORMAN

🌢 **A GOLDEN BOOK • NEW YORK**

Golden Books Publishing Company, Inc., New York, New York 10106

Three thousand years ago in the ancient city of Troy, there lived a handsome prince named Paris.

One day as Paris played his flute, three goddesses suddenly appeared before him: Aphrodite, the Guardian of Love; Athena, the Guardian of War; and Hera, Queen of the Immortals.

"We've come to ask your help," said Hera. "We can't decide which one of us is the fairest."

The immortals then gave him a golden apple on which was written: "To the Fairest."

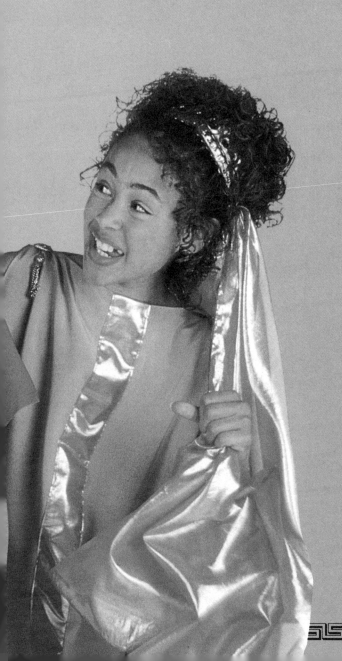

"All you have to do is hand the apple to the one who is the fairest," Athena explained to him. "Choose me and I will give you strength and wisdom."

"I offer unlimited wealth and power," Hera said.

Beautiful Aphrodite smiled and offered to help him win the heart of any girl he wanted.

After thinking about his options, Paris chose Aphrodite.

Aphrodite returned the golden apple to Paris. "Whoever you give this to will follow you to the ends of the earth," she told him.

Then, with a wave of her immortal hand, Aphrodite took Paris to the Greek city of Sparta. There he saw Helen, the queen of Sparta, the prettiest girl in the world.

Paris was smitten by Helen's beauty, but she was unimpressed with the prince.

However, once he handed her the apple, she fell
under its spell, and followed Paris back to Troy.

The Spartans were furious when they discovered their queen was gone. King Agamemnon raised a powerful army to rescue her from Paris.

Chief among the warriors was Odysseus the Wise, whose wits were even sharper than his sword; Zelda the Accurate, whose arrows never missed their mark; and Achilles the Invincible, the strongest warrior in all of Greece.

After a long and rough journey, the army finally landed on the shores of Troy.

They found the city surrounded by a 100-foot wall designed to keep intruders out. Odysseus knocked on the gate and demanded the return of Helen.

Paris and his general, Hektor, just laughed at him. They knew no one could get inside Troy's towering city walls.

"If you want Helen back, you're going to have to fight for her," Paris taunted.

And fight is just what the Spartans did. For nine long years both armies fought each other on the sunburnt fields outside the city of Troy.

During the tenth year, the Spartans began to weaken from hunger and too much fighting.

Zelda's eyes blurred with exhaustion, and she accidentally shot Odysseus with an arrow.

Agamemnon, who once had struck terror in the hearts of the Trojan troops, began to trip over his own spear.

And when challenged by Hektor, Achilles the Invincible suddenly lost his confidence and ran away in fear. The Spartans were in deep trouble. Odysseus necded to come up with an idea to end the war soon.

Odysseus proposed to Paris that the Spartans and the Trojans fight one more day, from sunup to sundown. Whoever was the victor at sunset would win the war and Helen.

Paris agreed, but on one condition: The battle would take place on the very next day, and the Spartans would have no chance to rest before the fight.

The Spartans didn't feel strong enough to fight, but Odysseus tried to rally his warriors. "We're all in this together," he reminded them.

On the battlefront, the Spartans fought with renewed strength. Agamemnon's sword sang through the air as Trojans fell at his dancing feet. Zelda wore her glasses and shot perfectly aimed arrows.

Suddenly Achilles appeared. He had been sitting in front of his tent, gathering his courage to fight. But when he remembered the encouraging words of his friends, he knew he could not let them down. Achilles challenged Hektor to a fight and won the battle!

At sundown the Trojans were losing the war but, instead of surrendering, they hid behind their city's walls. This meant the war could not end that day.

The Spartans needed to outsmart the Trojans. So clever Odysseus thought of another great plan. "We'll give the Trojans a gift and then sneak into their city," he declared.

Soon the whole Spartan army was hard at work building their gift—a giant wooden horse!

When the Trojan Horse was finished, the Spartans wheeled it to the gates of Troy.

Paris read out loud the parchment that was attached to the gift: *"Dear Trojans . . . We quit . . . You win . . . signed, the Spartans."*

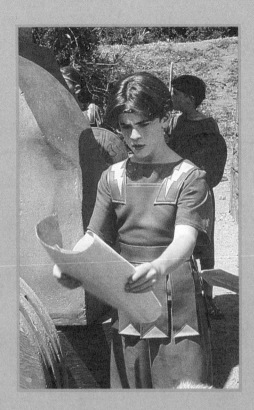

Hektor was suspicious, but Paris demanded that he help drag the horse into the city.

"People of Troy! Victory is ours!" Paris called to his people.

Skeptical Hektor guarded the horse, but by sunrise he was very sleepy.

Finally, all the Trojans were asleep. Suddenly, a trap door opened from the belly of the horse. The Spartans had been hiding inside! Quietly, they crept out of the horse and opened the city gates. Their army, led by Zelda and Agamemnon, marched into the city.

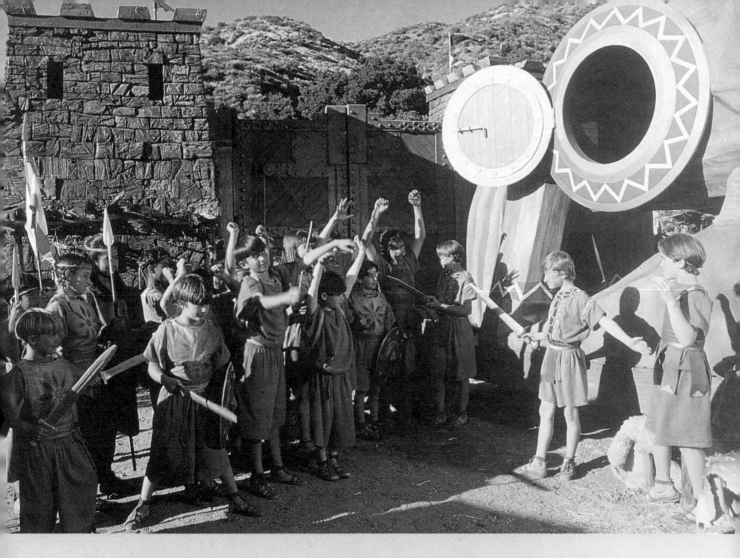

Paris awoke with a start and saw his warriors with their hands up in surrender. The Spartans had surrounded them.

"Morning, sweet prince," Odysseus said with a smirk as he pointed his sword at Paris.

The Trojan War was finally over—and the Spartans had won!

The Spartans had one last mission—to rescue
Queen Helen. She was still under the spell of
the golden apple. Odysseus took the apple from
her hand and let it fall to the ground.

At last the spell was broken!

"Where am I?" she asked.

"It's a long story," said Odysseus. He took
Helen by the arm and they all began the long
journey home.